A problem with the plan

* * *

"Suzette's *much* funner than Lulu," Hanni informed Alfie, as if explaining something everyone knew. "Lulu thinks she's so great," she added, shrugging.

Wait. That's kind of more like you, Alfie thought, her breath catching in her throat. What was happening to her secret plan that this really fun group of three girls—Hanni, Lulu, and herself—would be best friends forever?

They'd be perfect together!

"*Much* funner than Lulu," Hanni repeated in her bossiest, that's-that tone of voice. "So I'm gonna go find Suzette, right after I call dibs on the best desk."

"And then we'll find Lulu, too," Alfie added, as if that's what Hanni had been about to add. "Because she doesn't think she's so great. You'll really like her, Hanni. Once you get to know her better."

"Maybe," Hanni said over her shoulder as she pushed her way down the crowded hall.

Whoo, Alfie thought, her heart sinking as she headed after her.

This was going to be harder th̲ ̲ ̲ ̲ ̲ ̲ ̲

Books by Sally Warner

✻　✻　✻

THE ABSOLUTELY ALFIE SERIES

Absolutely Alfie and the Furry Purry Secret

Absolutely Alfie and the First Week Friends

Absolutely Alfie and the Worst Best Sleepover

THE ELLRAY JAKES SERIES

EllRay Jakes Is Not a Chicken!

EllRay Jakes Is a Rock Star!

EllRay Jakes Walks the Plank!

EllRay Jakes the Dragon Slayer!

EllRay Jakes and the Beanstalk

EllRay Jakes Is Magic!

EllRay Jakes Rocks the Holidays!

EllRay Jakes the Recess King!

EllRay Jakes Stands Tall!

THE EMMA SERIES

Only Emma

Not-So-Weird Emma

Super Emma

Best Friend Emma

Excellent Emma

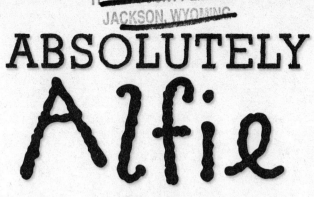

ABSOLUTELY Alfie

• and the •

FIRST WEEK FRIENDS

SALLY WARNER

illustrated by **SHEARRY MALONE**

PUFFIN BOOKS

PUFFIN BOOKS
An imprint of Penguin Random House LLC
375 Hudson Street
New York, New York 10014

Published simultaneously in the United States of America by Viking and Puffin Books,
imprints of Penguin Random House LLC, 2017

Text copyright © 2017 by Sally Warner
Illustrations copyright © 2017 by Shearry Malone

LIBRARY OF CONGRESS CATALOGING-IN-PUBLICATION DATA IS AVAILABLE

Puffin Books 9781101999912

Printed in the United States of America
Book design by Nancy Brennan

1   3   5   7   9   10   8   6   4   2

To my helpful second grade teacher friends:
Meliscent Peterson Gill, Signe Hanson,
and Laura Jackson Brophy —S.W.

To Mom and Dad—thank you for always
believing in me and paying for that art degree!
You're both the best. With love —S.M.

*   *   *

Contents

• • • • • • • • •

ABSOLUTELY Alfie

• and the •

FIRST WEEK FRIENDS

The Jitters

"Come on, Alfie," EllRay Jakes said to his seven-year-old sister. "Finish your dinner so we can clear the table and go upstairs. It's Sunday. Board game night. And it's my turn to choose."

It was late August, the night before the first day of school. Alfie was going to be in second grade, and eleven-year-old EllRay would be a sixth grader. It was his last year at Oak Glen Primary School, in Oak Glen, California.

EllRay had already announced that this year, he was going to *rule*.

"You don't have to eat everything, sweetie," their mom told Alfie. "But have another bite of chicken, at least. And some of those carrots. You have to keep up your strength."

"I absolutely cannot eat," Alfie said, making a face as she clutched her stomach. "I think maybe I'm getting sick. Tummy trouble, Mom," she added, her eyes wide.

"Yeah," EllRay said, pretending to be helpful. "Maybe Alfie should stay home tomorrow and watch TV all day. She can cuddle with Princess, and drink ginger ale, and eat grilled cheese sandwiches until she feels better."

Princess was their family's nine-week-old kitten. Alfie hated the thought of leaving her alone five days a week—just for *school*.

"Be quiet," she told her brother, swinging her foot in a wide arc under the dining table, trying to kick EllRay's long, skinny shin. "I mean it. My stomach really feels weird."

"That's called having the jitters," her mom explained. "It's like stage fright, and it's totally normal. Look, I know you're excited, Alfie," she added, her voice soft. "But there's nothing to be nervous about. Your school supplies are stacked on your desk," she said, holding up one slim brown finger as if she were counting. "And your new backpack is adorable. And your first-day outfit is all set and ready to go."

Three fingers were now in the air.

"Can they be ready to go without me, maybe?" Alfie asked—as if the darling T-shirt, flouncy short skirt, and leggings might be able to head out the door alone tomorrow morning. Her perfect new slip-on sneakers could lead the way.

Let *them* go to school if they wanted to so much, Alfie thought, making a face.

Let *them* meet the new kids in class, not to mention her new teacher.

Mr. Havens.

Mr. Havens was also called "Coach" at Oak Glen, because he taught some kids basketball during recess. Mostly boys and older girls.

"Why do I have to have a boy teacher this year?" Alfie almost wailed, asking no one in particular. "*Why me?*"

"Ha! You're lucky to have Coach," EllRay said, giving up on his little sister. He took his plate and silverware to the kitchen.

"And Coach Havens is a man, not a boy," her mother said.

"But he's too tall, Mom," Alfie tried to explain.

"He's so tall that I probably won't even be able to hear him when he talks. My grades will be terrible! And he'll probably like the boys in our class better than the girls. And—"

"And nothing, Miss Alfie," her mother said. "Now you're just being silly. And you're working yourself into a tizzy for no reason. This is your third year at Oak Glen Primary School, young lady. You will already know most of the kids in your class," she continued, starting another invisible list, this one a list of reasons why Alfie should not be having the jitters. "And now that you and Hanni are such pals," she added, "you'll have another friend to add to your posse."

"I'm not a cowboy or a rap star, Mom," Alfie objected. "I don't have a posse."

And wasn't it weird how the words "young lady" always meant trouble? It sounded like they should be a compliment, but *no*.

She *was* glad she and Hanni Sobel were now friends, however, Alfie admitted to herself. Hanni lived only one block away, and they were going to carpool together this year. She and Alfie had been in the same first grade class, but the girls weren't really friends until just a couple of weeks ago.

Hanni had wavy dark hair, green eyes, and cheeks that dimpled when she smiled. But she was also a little bit of a bossy, know-it-all kind of kid—though she actually did know it all, in Alfie's opinion.

And in Hanni's opinion, too.

She knew most of it, at least.

Alfie was glad to be starting school with Hanni on her side.

Not only that, but Alfie already had a best school friend from first grade, the always-cute Lulu Marino, though Lulu had been away all summer visiting relatives in Maine. So Alfie would be starting second grade with *two* good friends, because Hanni and Lulu were sure to like each other, right? Even though they had never hung out much together? After all, Alfie was friends with each of them.

So it just made sense that they would all get along.

Hanni was a leader.

Lulu's specialty was cuteness.

And Alfie had enough energy for the three of them.

It would be Alfie's second grade wish come true.

The three of them were going to have *so much fun* together! In fact, their friendship was Alfie's first week, second grade wish. Her *friend plan*. After all, didn't all the best things come in groups of three?

There were the famous three little kittens who lost their mittens, Alfie thought, tossing a tiny piece of chicken under the table, hoping Princess was there.

And what about the three billy goats gruff? Not that she planned to be gruff.

And how about Wynken, Blynken, and Nod? Whoever they were.

And—there were last summer's s'mores, Alfie reminded herself, her mouth watering. They were so good that you always wanted some more. S'more.

Graham crackers, marshmallows, and chocolate. *Mmm.*

Three perfect ingredients—just like Hanni, Lulu, and herself.

Alfie looked down at the remaining chicken and carrots on her plate.

"Two more bites of each," her mother told her. "And sweetie, you know second grade is going to be *so much fun,*" she added, as if she had been listening in on Alfie's silent conversation with herself.

How did her mom do that?

"Come *on,*" EllRay was urging from the doorway. Tall and thin, he was tapping one of his giant sneakered feet like he meant business.

"Okay," Alfie told him. "But will Dad be home in time to tuck me in for good luck?" she asked her mom, shoving the carrots around with her fork before popping two slices into her mouth and washing them down with some milk.

Dr. Jakes taught geology at a college in San Diego, about an hour's drive away.

But he often spent Sunday evenings at a local

gym. It was the best weekend time for him to exercise.

Alfie's dad was not a medical doctor. But people also got to be called "doctor" when they completed the highest level of study in their field, Alfie had learned.

"He will be home by bedtime for sure," her mom said, nodding. "But your father believes in hard work and science, not luck," she couldn't help but add.

"I know," Alfie said after swallowing her last required bite of chicken. "But *I'm* the one who has to start second grade tomorrow, Mom," she added. "And I'm gonna need all the luck I can get."

Three Perfect Ingredients

"Oof. Here we go," Hanni said, peering out the car window as Mrs. Sobel pulled up in front of the school the next morning. Mrs. Sobel's long earrings dangled beneath the perfect straight edges of her hair. Sitting behind her in the back seat, Alfie felt as though she'd been hypnotized by those earrings.

Hanni sounded nervous, she thought, surprised.

Hanni Sobel, who had tried to be the boss of the girls in first grade.

Hanni, "the world's oldest seven-year-old," according to Alfie's mom.

Hanni had the jitters, too!

"It's okay," Alfie heard herself telling Hanni. "It's gonna be a really good year."

"It definitely is," Mrs. Sobel agreed, reaching around to give her daughter's knee a squeeze. "Now, Alfie's mom will be picking you up at three-fifteen. Don't keep her waiting, ladies."

"We won't," the girls said together. Then each took a deep breath and got out of the car.

Alfie stared at the bustling scene spread before her like she was watching a movie. Her school

looked different, as if it had changed in some small, mysterious way over the summer.

It was a brand-new year, and anything could happen! Alfie guessed that was it.

"Let's go find Lulu Marino," Alfie said as she and Hanni headed up the crowded steps leading to the school's wide front door.

"Why?" Hanni asked, waving at Principal James, who prided himself on knowing each kid's name.

"Hello, Hanni Sobel and Alfie Jakes," Principal James called out, looking as if he had just checked off two names from an invisible list.

"I think we should find our classroom first," Hanni told Alfie. "We can peek in and make sure no one has grabbed the best desks yet. Because I want first dibs."

Hanni was definitely a first-dibs kind of girl, Alfie thought, hiding a smile. "I'm pretty sure Mr. Havens's class will be on the first floor," she said. "And still locked."

Oak Glen Primary School liked to keep the youngest kids away from the stairs at either end of the long central corridor, she knew. "Upstairs is for fourth, fifth, and sixth-graders only," EllRay had informed her over the summer. "It's so you little guys don't mess everything up by falling down the stairs and wrecking the traffic flow."

"And anyway," Alfie continued as they passed the school office, "Mr. Havens is probably the type of teacher who tells kids exactly where to sit."

She remembered Mr. Havens—"Coach"—barking orders on the playground during recess and knew she was right.

"Listen up!"

"Okay, go."

"Think fast!"

"Hup, hup!"

Around them in the hall, clusters of older girls were hugging and telling each other how good they looked. They talked fast, as if there was no way they could possibly catch up on enough of each others' news before school started.

A few worried-looking kindergartners were hanging back, clinging to their moms or dads. They clearly wanted to return home instead of starting school. Alfie felt sorry for them. "I'm over it!" she heard one little boy yell.

The gleaming hall smelled like fruity shampoo and floor polish.

Some of the older boys, having already locked their bikes or skateboards in the pen in the corner of the playground, joked in loud voices. They shoved each other in a friendly way, for the most part, as they roared their greetings up and down the hall.

"Yo, dude!"

"Dawg."

"Wassup, bro?"

Alfie thought she heard her brother's voice in the raucous, ear-ringing mix, but she couldn't be sure. She felt homesick for EllRay for a second.

"Anyway," Hanni was saying as loud as she could, "why would I want to go looking for Lulu when I haven't seen Suzette since the Fourth of July?"

"Huh? Suzette *Monahan*?" Alfie asked, frowning. She liked Suzette okay. She had known her since their preschool days at Oak Glen's Kreative Learning and Daycare. But she and Suzette didn't hang out much anymore.

It was no big deal, they just didn't.

{ 14 }

"Suzette's *much* funner than Lulu," Hanni informed Alfie, as if explaining something everyone knew. "Lulu thinks she's so great," she added, shrugging.

Wait. That's kind of more like you, Alfie thought, her breath catching in her throat. What was happening to her secret plan that this really fun group of three girls—Hanni, Lulu, and herself—would be best friends forever?

They'd be perfect together!

"*Much* funner than Lulu," Hanni repeated in her bossiest, that's-that tone of voice. "So I'm gonna go find Suzette, right after I call dibs on the best desk."

"And then we'll find Lulu, too," Alfie added, as if that's what Hanni had been about to add. "Because she doesn't think she's so great. You'll really like her, Hanni. Once you get to know her better."

"Maybe," Hanni said over her shoulder as she pushed her way down the crowded hall.

Whoo, Alfie thought, her heart sinking as she headed after her.

This was going to be harder than she'd thought!

All-Stars

"Listen up and settle down, All-Stars," Mr. Havens called out from his great height as the second graders churned into the classroom once the door was open. "Stow all your gear in the cubby room, then look for your name tags on the tables and sit down. And *no switching places*," he warned. "I have a chart."

Tables this year, not desks.

Five tables sat so that everyone could see Mr. Haven's desk if they tried. There were two tables on each side and one in the back. Two kids were to sit on each side of the table, and one at the end. A plastic container of supplies sat at the other end.

This is different, Alfie thought, biting her lip. *Huh.*

She shoved her backpack into an empty cubby. She adjusted the ruffles on her new skirt as if that might make things feel more normal.

Mr. Havens looked more dressed-up than Alfie remembered from last year, she noted in surprise before searching the spotless tables for her name tag. It was as if he, too, had made an effort to look nice this first day of school.

Teachers did that?

He was even wearing a suit jacket over his shirt, Alfie saw. And he'd gotten a really short haircut. Prickles of bristly hair glittered on the almost-shaved sides of his big, bony head, a head that looked like it had actual muscles on it. Was that even possible?

"Dude! We're the All-Stars," one boy was saying, fist-bumping another boy. "This year is gonna be *awesome*."

"Our first grade class was called the Dolphins," Alfie heard Suzette tell Hanni. "Remember? In the good old days? At least dolphins are smart."

Suzette's light brown hair had grown so long that it now fell over her shoulders, Alfie saw. *That lucky*, she thought.

"I liked being a Dolphin," Lulu Marino agreed. But Suzette and Hanni didn't seem to hear her speak.

"We were the Otters at my old school," another girl said. "And they're the cutest animals in the world! You should see them. I don't even know what All-Stars *are*."

"It's got something to do with sports," Alfie's old preschool friend Arletty Jackson said. She had brown skin like Alfie, as did three other kids in their new class.

"Sports." "Sports!" a few girls whispered to each other, alarmed. A lot of them liked sports, Alfie knew—including her. But not team sports, except soccer. Not yet.

And Mr. Havens was obviously a team sports kind of guy.

"Yeah," Hanni said. "But 'All-Stars'? *Everybody* can't be a star," she pointed out, her arms folding across her chest as if she was getting up the nerve to break the news to Mr. Havens. "My mom always says that somebody has to be the best," she continued, chin up. "Or else the world doesn't make any sense. *All-Stars*," she repeated, shaking her head. "We should have gotten to vote on our class name."

"Yeah, vote," Suzette agreed. "*And* we have to sit at stupid tables," she added. "It's like being kindergarten babies all over again."

"And my back is facing the teacher," Hanni almost wailed, spotting her name tag. "I'll have to turn around just to see him! I'm *doomed*. How am I gonna come in first if he never notices me?"

Not much chance of him not noticing her! But Alfie was at the same table as Hanni. *Phew*, she thought, relieved. So at least part of her plan was working out.

"Gross," a boy at their table teased. "Hanni just said her back has a face on it." Scooter Davis, Alfie remembered. He was in her first grade class last year.

"Change places with me," Hanni said to Alfie, ignoring Scooter.

"We're not supposed to," Alfie said. "Mr. Havens has a *chart*."

Arletty was at their table too. She had been assigned the spot at the end of the table. Scooter and a shy new boy named Alan Lewis filled the other two seats.

But at least Lulu was at the table just behind them, Alfie was happy to see. And she looked cute, too. Getting her and Hanni together for their magical group of three shouldn't be too hard, she thought, giving Lulu a secret wave.

Not too hard for an All-Star like her!

"Listen," Hanni was telling Arletty, who was about to sit down. "You're sitting at the end of the table, but that doesn't mean you're the boss or anything. Because we haven't decided yet. Okay?" She smiled at Arletty as if that might take the sting out of her words.

Hey, Alfie thought, frowning. That wasn't very nice. Arletty never did anything bad to anyone, and now this? Hanni wasn't usually so in-your-face.

"Um," Alfie began, trying to think of what to say to Hanni, and how to say it.

"Okay," Arletty was already assuring Hanni. The pretty beads on her braids clicked as she nodded her head.

"Anyway, who made you the queen of our table, Hanni?" Scooter Davis asked, eager to face off with the girl. A chunk of dark blond hair flopped onto his forehead.

"Mind your own business, *Scooter*," Hanni told him.

"Rears in chairs, All-Stars, and name tags on your chests," Mr. Havens said, his outdoors coach-voice cutting through the kids' noise like a chain-saw slicing through strawberry ice cream. "You're in 'the bigs' this year, second-graders. And if you haven't found your name tags by now, we will have ourselves some problems."

They already *had* some problems, Alfie thought, trying to ignore both Hanni and Scooter as she slid into her chair.

For example, these new tables were different—and weird.

And there were more boys than girls in her class.

And Lulu Marino was sitting at a different table from Hanni and her.

And Arletty Jackson looked like she was about to cry.

And Scooter and Hanni were already "butting heads," as Alfie's mom would say.

And Hanni Sobel—her newest friend—was acting nervous and a little mean.

Also, Hanni was mad at her for not switching seats.

And class hadn't even started yet! Not officially.

"Welcome, All-Stars," Mr. Havens said, beaming.

Icebreaker Time!

"Mr. Havens! Mr. Havens!" Hanni Sobel's hand shot up a moment after the teacher had finished taking attendance and introducing the second-grade kids who were new to Oak Glen Primary School.

But Alfie secretly thought that all kids—even the returning students—were at least a little bit new when school started each year. *She* felt new, anyway.

And once she got Hanni and Lulu together, the three of them would be best friends forever. That would be new, too.

"Yes, Hanni?" Mr. Havens asked with only a quick glance at her name tag.

"What are 'the bigs'?" Hanni asked, a frown on

her face. "You said we're *in* them, only I don't know what they are. And I don't wanna fall behind."

"Fair question," Mr. Havens told her, nodding. "'The bigs' is an expression used in professional sports. It means someone is playing in the major leagues. They're in the big-time. Like in baseball, for instance," he said. "Only in this case, I was using it as a way of saying that your serious education is beginning *now*, in second grade. That's my opinion, anyway."

"But what if we don't know anything *about* baseball?" Hanni asked, still worried.

"You don't need to," Mr. Havens assured her. "But we can all learn more about each other, can't we? And today is the perfect day to do it. Icebreaker time!"

"Icebreaker?" Lulu Marino asked without raising her hand. Her straight brown hair shone under the fluorescent lights.

"I use my hind teeth for breaking ice," Scooter informed everyone.

"In this case, an 'icebreaker' is just something fun to do," Mr. Havens explained after giving both Lulu and Scooter a look. "It's something—like a game—that will help people get to know each other better."

Are we gonna need a translator in this class? Alfie asked herself.

"So, gather around, everyone," Mr. Havens was saying. "Sit in a curved line in front of my desk so we can all see one another."

"On the *bare floor*? In my *new clothes*?" Suzette Monahan exclaimed, sounding as if Mr. Havens had just asked her to scrub the art sink in her best party dress.

"This is terrible," Hanni murmured, shaking her head to show how sorry she was for her friend.

"You must come to school ready to work," Mr. Havens told everyone, pointing here and there to get them settled on the floor. "This isn't a fashion show—or a drama academy, Miss Monahan," he added, seeing the face Suzette was making. "Sit on a piece of notebook paper if you must."

"I *will*," Suzette said, grabbing one from the container of supplies at the end of her table. She settled onto it carefully, looking like a small angry chicken about to lay an egg.

Mr. Havens perched on the front of his desk, facing the arc of second graders with a welcoming smile. He was now holding a colorful striped beach ball that seemed to have appeared out of nowhere. There was black printing on its shiny curved sides.

"*Boo-ya!* Think fast. Catch," Mr. Havens said, tossing the ball to Scooter Davis.

The second-graders were startled but excited by this unexpected event. What was happening?

"Tell us who you are," Mr. Havens said to Scooter. "And then please answer the question that your right hand is touching on the ball."

"Okay," Scooter said, sounding eager to take part. "My name is Scooter Davis," Scooter said. "My real name is Stephen, only nobody calls me that unless I'm in trouble. And..." He looked down at his hand on the ball. "And my favorite thing to eat is caramel popcorn," he finished, grinning.

"Thank you, Scooter," Mr. Havens said. "Very nourishing indeed. Now, throw the ball to someone else. *Gently*," he added, before Scooter could spike it hard at someone's head, shouting, *"Think fast!"*

Because that was Scooter's way. Alfie knew this from first grade experience.

"Boo-ya!"

Alfie thought the new girl holding the beach ball was probably wishing she was back at her old school right about now. "Oh," the girl exclaimed, her cheeks turning pink as everyone looked at her. "Okay. My name is Phoebe Miller, and I don't have any other name. Even when I'm in trouble. And my favorite color is lime green, only my mom says it looks funny on me. So I can't wear it."

Wow! Alfie was glad her mom didn't say mean stuff like that to *her*.

"Thanks, Phoebe," Mr. Havens said. "Did you recently move to Oak Glen?"

"Three weeks ago," Phoebe said, nodding. "From Wickenburg, Arizona."

"It's pretty hot in Arizona," Mr. Havens said. "Now, pass the ball."

"Can I roll it?" Phoebe asked, her straight blonde hair already swinging as she prepared to do just that. Phoebe was really pretty, Alfie thought.

"Try tossing it," Mr. Havens said. "And give us a *'boo-ya,'* Phoebe."

Phoebe choked out the goofy words as she threw the ball to another kid.

Meanwhile, Alfie was practicing what she was going to say when it was *her* turn to speak. She would tell everyone that her name was Alfie, which most of them already knew, including Mr. Havens. But she would *not* tell them that her real name was "Alfleta," or that it meant "beautiful elf" in Old Saxon, a language no one had spoken for more than a thousand years.

Her romance-writing mom had come up with that one. *Thanks, Mom.*

And if she could manage it, Alfie promised herself, the answer to her beach ball question would include the thrilling news that she had a brand-new kitten at home named Princess! She knew she could work it in. *"My favorite food is cheese, only not the stinky kind. And my brand-new kitten named Princess loves cheese, too."*

Score!

Mr. Havens cleared his throat. "We're supposed to be *listening*, people, not just waiting for our own turn to talk," he told everyone. But Alfie thought he might have been glancing at her when he said it. "Remember that advice your whole life long," he continued. "But especially today, because there may be a little quiz before lunch about your fellow classmates, with prizes involved."

A chorus of whispers filled the room. *"A quiz?"* *"Prizes?"*

"What did you say your favorite color was?" Scooter asked Phoebe.

"This semester is going to be all about teamwork," Mr. Havens continued, his booming voice quashing their excited squeaks. "Got that? *Team-work*. I'll be explaining that to your parents and guardians on Friday, at Back to School Night. But to be a good team member, you have to learn to listen, and not just flap your gums. Listen to even the quietest voice on your team."

Another boy's hand was in the air, and Mr. Havens called on him. "Because there is no 'I' in *team*, right, Coach?" the boy asked, as if he already knew the answer.

"That's right, Mr. Martinez," Mr. Havens said. "There's just *T - E - A - M*. But I'm 'Mr. Havens' in here, Bryan," he added. "Not Coach."

"Okay, Coach," Bryan said, almost saluting, he was so eager to please.

What in the world were they talking about? Alfie did not have a clue.

But she started listening better from that point on.

Because—*prizes*!

An Unexpected
Problem

"That worksheet was way too easy," Hanni said on their way out to recess the next morning, Tuesday.

It was nearly the last day of August, and it was hot, hot, hot outside—even at ten in the morning. But Mr. Havens's second graders were eager for a break from class. They needed to *move*.

Hanni's complaint about the worksheet was like a piece of pie, Alfie couldn't help but think, picturing it as her tummy growled. Pie with some whipped cream–bragging on top.

Hanni was complicated that way. But she could also be nice, Alfie knew.

Hanni was quick to play any game of let's-pretend that Alfie could invent.

{ 31 }

And she was really good—better than Alfie!—at sharing her toys and dolls.

And she and Alfie had made a very cool fairy-land next to the Sobels' fishpond.

Also, Hanni had given Alfie Princess—*and* helped make her some cute kitty toys.

"Yeah, but they cheated on it," Scooter said over his shoulder. "The worksheet, I mean."

"Who cheated? Who is 'they'?" Suzette asked, jumping in to defend Hanni—not that Hanni need-ed defending. "The worksheet cheated?" she went on. "Because worksheets can't cheat. They're just pieces of paper. And it was a 'Two-Syllable Word Search,' *Stephen*," she said, not giving up. "All you had to do was find the two-syllable words Mr. Ha-vens has been teaching us, and then draw a circle around them."

"Not really a circle," Lulu said, chiming in. "More like a long, skinny blob."

"But one of my right answers got marked wrong," Scooter said, not backing down. "And it's a real word. 'App.' So that's cheating."

"'App' isn't two syllables, though, Scooter," Alfie

pointed out, careful to use the name he preferred. "I think we were supposed to circle the word 'apple,' not just the 'app' part."

"Or blob it," Lulu said.

"'App' is two syllables if you say it slow enough," Scooter argued. *"A-a-a-p-p-p-p,"* he demonstrated, drawing out the word.

He was not going to give this a rest, Alfie told herself, sighing.

"It could even be *three* syllables, if you say it that good," Bryan Martinez agreed, nodding. "Dude, you should have got extra credit!"

"Dumb test," Scooter said.

It was a worksheet, not a test, Alfie wanted to remind the boys. But she had other things on her mind. It was the first week of school, and this Tuesday morning recess was the perfect time to get Hanni and Lulu together. And then their group of three would be complete—and Alfie's first week, second grade plan would be come true, she thought, smiling.

Any later in the week and it could be too late. Second grade girls' friendships could harden into place fast. Those friendships might be like papier mâché Alfie thought, remembering a summer craft project she'd done at Little Acorns Day Camp. And once papier mâché started to dry, you could not change things around. You could add stuff, sure. But the basic shape was just *there*.

And she wanted *her* basic shape to be a triangle: Hanni, Lulu, and her, Alfie. Leadership, cuteness, and energy. The perfect combination. The perfect *team*.

It was something they could only achieve *together*.

But Hanni, Suzette, and that new girl Phoebe were already heading toward the chain link fence behind the picnic tables, a popular girls' hangout.

"Listen, Lulu," Alfie said at their picnic table while they were rooting around in their snack bags, hoping for the best. "Let's *us* go hang out by the fence too, okay? With Hanni and Suzette and that new girl?"

"Her name's Phoebe. And it's too hot over

there," Lulu said between dainty bites of cracker. "No shade. I don't want to get all sweaty and sunburned."

The playground *was* seeming to wobble in the heat, Alfie saw, gazing across its expanse. And like Suzette, Lulu was very fussy about her clothes. About everything, to be honest. About her long, shiny hair. Her perfectly straight bangs. Lulu's mother called her "my special darling," they'd all been informed last year—something Alfie could not imagine her own mom saying with a straight face.

She wouldn't mind hearing it at least once, though.

"*I'll* come with you, Alfie," Arletty piped up from the other side of the table. "I like Phoebe."

"I like her too," Alfie protested. "I mean, she *seems* okay."

It was just that Phoebe wasn't the point, Alfie thought.

But why *not* let Arletty come with them to the fence? She was pretty cool, Alfie reminded herself. Arletty was often too busy for play-dates on weekends because of church-related activities. But she could be lots of fun. And Arletty was also an old daycare friend. "Okay, sure," she told Arletty. "But Lulu, you absolutely gotta come with us. Because—"

"Because why?" Lulu interrupted, licking cracker salt off her fingers. "My mom says I should take it easy when it's this hot out."

"Take it easy" had never been one of Alfie Jakes's mottos, that was for sure! She liked to jump around too much for that. Maybe not on a shimmery-hot day like today, she admitted to herself. But her dad didn't call her "Cricket" for nothing.

Why was she just sitting here?

You're working on your plan, that's why, Alfie reminded herself.

"Listen, Lulu," she said, trying another approach. "You just *have* to come with us to the fence. I think Hanni has a secret she wants to tell you."

She was making up the lie on the spot!

"Huh," Lulu said, making a face and shaking her head at the same time. "It's probably just some so-called secret about how she wants to boss me around—like she did all last year. No, thank you."

This was unexpected, Alfie thought, biting her lower lip. It was an obstacle to her plan. And she was running out of time!

"Hanni *can* be kinda bossy," Arletty reminded Alfie. "You gotta admit."

"But she never means it in a bad way," Alfie

told both Arletty and Lulu. "She gave me my kitty, Princess, after all," she pointed out. "And people can change. Right?"

"My dad says people *can* change, but they usually don't want to," Lulu informed them all.

"But they can," Alfie repeated, picking out the good part of Lulu's sentence.

"But they usually don't want to," Lulu said again. "And I don't want to get heat stroke and wreck my outfit when I faint on the boiling-hot playground," she added. Lulu Marino wore outfits, Alfie reminded herself. Other kids just wore clothes.

Of course, Lulu didn't seem to have as much *fun* as the other kids, but—

"So we're not going over to the fence?" Arletty asked, sounding disappointed.

"I guess not," Alfie said. "Anyway, recess is almost over."

"Well, 'recess' is a two-syllable word," Arletty announced, jumping to her feet. "So I'm gonna go *play*, you guys. Just sitting and eating isn't any fun. Not once you're full, anyways."

Alfie agreed with Arletty about playing during recess. Wasn't that the whole point?

Her legs needed to run!

But Alfie wanted to stay on Lulu's sweet side. She had to, because even though things were not looking good right now, she, Alfie Jakes, had not given up.

My plan *is gonna rule*, she vowed silently to no one in particular. *You'll see!*

6

The Assignment

"Listen up and settle down," Mr. Havens told his class half an hour before school was to let out that afternoon. "Today is Tuesday, All-Stars. And Back to School Night is on Friday. That's just three more days. Back to School Night is for parents and guardians only," he reminded them.

As if kids would want to come traipsing back to school at night after making it through the first week! Alfie stopped herself just in time from shaking her head in amazement at the very idea.

Her mom and dad would get a sitter for her and EllRay the way they did last year. Bree, probably.

She and her brother might even get to order pizza and watch a movie!

Not a scary one, though.

"I'll be putting up some of your work around the room," Mr. Havens was saying. "Including those drawing and writing papers I had you do this afternoon."

This is how I look today! And this is how I sign my name! Alfie remembered, wondering if she'd made her hair cute enough in the drawing.

She hadn't known it was going to be on display.

"I'll be telling our guests about the rules and regulations," Mr. Havens continued. "So that everyone is on the same page, so to speak. And I'll tell them that this semester is going to be all about teamwork. In class, on the playground. *Teamwork.* And I asked myself, what better way would there be to demonstrate teamwork than with examples of group projects arranged all around the classroom? Like an art show?"

Alfie wondered if Mr. Havens really talked to himself that way. Her conversations with herself were more like, *"Chocolate."*

And, *"Where did I hide that dollar Auntie sent me?"*

And, *"Is EllRay still hogging the bathroom?"*

And, *"I wish I had silver shoes like that girl I saw at Target."*

And, *"Do I smell tacos?"*

And, *"How come there have to be mosquitos?"*

And—*"Chocolate!"*

Mr. Havens's twenty-five students stared at him, their expressions a blend of alarm and confusion. How were they supposed to provide examples of teamwork on Friday night when they had just been ordered to stay home?

"The assignment I have in mind will serve two purposes," Mr. Havens went on, looking pleased with himself. "First, the artwork you do this week will show the value of teamwork. It will be a beginning, at least. And second, when your finished pieces are arranged together, they will provide really cool decorations for the classroom on the big night. Because I am supposed to decorate, I'm told," he added under his breath.

What kind of artwork was he talking about?

"You'll be divided into groups of four or five," Mr. Havens said. "I've already chosen the teams, and there will be no switching. This project is kind of an experiment," he confessed, laughing.

"So that makes it fun for me, too. Now, tomorrow and the day after tomorrow, Wednesday and Thursday, each group will work on this assignment together, as a team," he explained. "But don't worry. There will be a parent helper here to assist you each day."

The moment Mr. Havens said "don't worry," Alfie started worrying.

"Wednesday will be building day," Mr. Havens went on, "and Thursday will be decorating day. We will have an art exhibit in class on Friday afternoon to show off the finished projects," he added. "Maybe we'll invite the kindergartners—and our principal! I'm calling the assignment the Cardboard Challenge, and you're going to *love* it."

Love it? Alfie doubted that.

Maybe she'd love it, and maybe she wouldn't.

After all, she and Hanni had tried building a kitty climbing tower for Princess out of cardboard boxes and duct tape just a couple of weeks ago, and things had not gone well. Nothing stuck right, and she and Hanni argued the whole time they worked on it.

Fail!

"Mrs. Havens and I have been saving cardboard boxes all summer long," Mr. Havens continued. "Different sizes, flat sheets of cardboard, tubes, tiny boxes, and so on," he said. "Just all kinds of cardboard. And you'll be using paint and markers on your projects, too. Or you can decorate your cardboard with collage or glitter. Whatever you want, but as a *team*."

"*Glitter*," Alfie heard Lulu say from the table behind hers. Lulu loved shiny things.

"I'll be in charge of the paper cutter and the hot glue gun back in the craft closet," Mr. Havens informed them. "But you'll do the rest—with our parent helper. And you can build *something*," he continued, "such as a vehicle or a building. Or you can build *nothing*. Just construct a three-dimensional design."

"What's that mean?" Scooter said, raising his hand after he asked the question.

"'Three-dimensional' means length, width, and depth, Scooter," Mr. Havens explained. "Like a sculpture. In other words, it's not flat, like a drawing on a piece of paper. Paper is two-dimensional, just length and width. But a sculpture is something you can stub your toe on. Think of it that way, if it helps."

Alfie's head was starting to spin, because—what if the two-dimensional piece of paper got all crumpled up? Wouldn't that make it *three*-dimensional?

Could something be two different things at the same time?

And she didn't *want* to stub her toe—on anything.

"I'll announce the teams now, before the buzzer sounds," Mr. Havens was saying, glancing up at the clock. "So your teams can start talking about the projects tomorrow. And then you'll get together after lunch to start work on your structures. You will have two days to complete them."

And then he started reading off lists of names.

Alfie's team was last. "Alfie Jakes," Mr. Havens read aloud as kids started getting ready for the buzzer to sound. "Lulu Marino. Scooter Davis. And Hanni Sobel."

Alfie could hardly believe her luck. A miracle had happened! Mr. Havens had accidentally done her the biggest favor in the world. He had put Hanni and Lulu and her on the *same team*.

Her first week, second grade wish was coming true!

Sure, Scooter was part of the team too, but who cared? He would be outnumbered three-to-one by the girls.

And if he got in the way, she could always sneak in a bag of caramel popcorn to distract him, Alfie told herself, smiling.

That should keep him busy.

Two Homeworks

Alfie peeked around the corner of her brother's bedroom door after dinner that night. EllRay was hunched over his desk. "What are you doing?" Alfie asked.

"What do you think I'm doing?" EllRay said. "It's a school night. Homework."

"What kind of homework?" Alfie asked, easing into his room.

"Multiplying fractions," EllRay said.

"What's a fraction?" Alfie asked. "I forget."

"It's, like, part of something," EllRay told her. "Part of a number, in this case."

Alfie thought for a second. "But how can a number be part of another number?" she asked. "It would just be a different number, wouldn't it?"

She was starting to worry—four years in advance.

Sixth grade sounded hard!

"And how come you have to multiply them?" she went on. "Adding them up a whole bunch of times would be easier, right?"

"Yeah, but we added fractions last year," EllRay said.

He didn't seem bothered at being interrupted.

In fact, he looked almost grateful, Alfie noticed.

"Well, I have *two* homeworks," she told him, sitting down cross-legged on the shaggy rug next to his desk.

"I told you Mr. Havens would be hard," EllRay said, smiling. "Whatcha got?"

"First, I have arithmetic, like you," Alfie said. "Only we have these drawings of coins. We're supposed to add them up. But I'd rather have dollars," she said after thinking about it for a second.

"Me too," EllRay said, laughing. "What's your number two homework?"

"It's not exactly *homework*," Alfie told him. "It's more like I'm trying to come up with an idea for this teamwork project Mr. Havens says we gotta do. It's for Back to School Night on Friday. But I really need your help."

"What kind of project is it?" he asked, sounding half-interested.

"It's called the Cardboard Challenge," Alfie told him. "See, over the summer, Mr. Havens and Mrs. Havens saved up lots of junk for us to use. And we're supposed to make something out of the junk, then decorate it. There are three other kids on my team," she told her brother. "And we gotta work together—with Mr. Havens and our parent helper. But two of the kids are perfect team members for me," she reported, smiling.

Hanni and Lulu. Her wish come true!

Scooter was another story, but she could handle *him*.

"And you're the leader?" EllRay asked, frowning as he tried to sort out all this information.

"Nuh-uh," she said, shaking her head. "We don't *have* a leader. But I'm trying to figure out what we should make. That way, I can, like, *hint* it to everyone tomorrow."

"Hint it to everyone," EllRay echoed, looking blank.

"Because if I come up with something good enough," Alfie told him, "they'll all want to do it, and nobody will fight."

"Nobody will fight," EllRay repeated, though he sounded doubtful.

"Okay. So Mr. Havens said our project could

be something real, like a house," Alfie told her brother. "Or it could just be a beautiful made-up design. So, what should we do?"

"What materials do you have to work with?" EllRay asked after taking a peek at the robot clock on his bedroom wall. "What kind of cardboard stuff, I mean?"

"We haven't gotten anything yet," his sister told him. "So I don't know. We'll get it tomorrow."

"Then how can you plan your project tonight?" EllRay asked. "*Geez.*"

"*Geez,* yourself," Alfie told him. "My homework's not any weirder than multiplying little parts of nothing, EllRay. Anyway, this is like *secret* homework," she tried to explain. "It's not on a worksheet or anything. But I know you can help me with it. You've been on lots of teams before, right?" she asked. "You've made tons of cardboard stuff, too. And you know Mr. Havens. And I want our team to *win.*"

"It doesn't sound like this is supposed to be a contest," EllRay said.

"But there's gonna be an art show on Friday

afternoon, before Back to School Night," Alfie said. "Of course it's a contest. Hanni's mom thinks *everything* is a contest, Hanni says."

"I don't think that's right," EllRay argued, shaking his head.

Alfie could feel her face getting hot. "So you won't even *help* me?" she asked.

"Don't get all mad," EllRay said, holding up his hand.

"But I wanted to get a head start," Alfie cried. "Don't you want me to do good in second grade?"

"I want you to do *well*," her brother said. "That's what Mom and Dad would say, anyway. But you can't plan a project like this until you see the stuff you have to work with."

"But by then, then nobody will listen to me," Alfie said. "You were my last hope, EllRay!"

"Well, sorry to disappoint you," EllRay told her.

"And you're in the *sixth grade*," Alfie said, her voice scornful. "Thanks a lot."

"You're welcome a lot," EllRay said, turning back to his work. He was already drifting back to the land of fractions.

Alfie jumped to her feet, furious. Her big brother wasn't even going to look at her when she stormed out of his room? "See if I help *you* some day," she said.

"Good-bye, Alfie," EllRay told her, clearly taking pains to keep his voice calm. "Shut the door, please. And don't let it hit your booty on the way out."

"Shut the door yourself, if you love it so much," Alfie said, happy to be having the last word. "And quit saying 'your booty,' or I'm gonna tell. Sixth grader," she added, stomping her foot. "Big brother. *Hah!*"

Who's the Boss?

Wednesday lunch was going to be spent in the cafeteria, not outside, most of Mr. Havens's second grade kids agreed. It was the last day of August, and it was weird-hot outside.

That's how her unhelpful big brother would put it, Alfie remembered, wrestling her lunch out of her backpack. "Southern California has hot days," EllRay had explained to her more than once. "Then there are hot-hot days, when you can still kinda do stuff. But there are some weird-hot days every year, like one hundred five degrees or more, when you can't do anything except stay inside until it gets dark, almost."

EllRay wasn't right about *everything*, Alfie told herself as she and the rest of the kids made their way down the hall toward the air-conditioned cafeteria. But he was right about this.

Oak Glen Primary School's cafeteria and auditorium were in a sprawling, single-story building on the other side of the main school building, just past the office. A breezeway connected the two structures, but there wasn't much breeze today. Even the playground looked gooey and soft in this heat, Alfie thought, shuddering. She patted her pocket to make sure her milk money was still there. She was thirsty.

"Wait up," she called out to Hanni, who was striding along the breezeway as if she was in an invisible race—or on her way to a very important business meeting.

"Hurry up, slowpoke," Hanni said over her shoulder. But she was smiling with some of last summer's old friendliness. Alfie sighed with relief.

Now, all she had to do was get smiling-Hanni together with Lulu, who was wearing a really cute dress with hearts on it today. Then her first week, second grade plan might still come true. And lunch was the perfect time for it to happen!

"Where do you wanna sit?" she asked Hanni after they had grabbed their square, waxy cartons of milk from an ice-filled bin and paid for them.

The aroma of spicy taco meat mixed in the air with dish soap and disinfectant. It was a familiar smell to Alfie. It reminded her of her first grade cafeteria days. Things were so easy back then, she thought—when there hadn't been a plan she needed to make come true.

The cafeteria was extra-crowded today, of course, because both the kids who were buying lunch and the kids who had brought their lunches from home were jammed into the big room together. But Alfie and Hanni squeezed in next to Lulu and Phoebe. Phoebe was on a different team from theirs, Alfie remembered.

"You guys," Lulu said to Hanni and Alfie. "We're working on our cardboard project right after lunch. And that boy Scooter Davis is probably gonna try to boss us around."

"There are two boys on my team," Phoebe reported, as if she had dared herself to take part in the conversation. "At least you only have one boy."

"But he thinks he's so great," Hanni said as she peeled apart her sandwich to inspect what was inside.

"Do you really think Scooter is that bad?" Alfie asked, frowning as she thought about it. True, Scooter had been kind of a rowdy guy at recess when they were in first grade. But he was older now. And she liked him better after Monday's icebreaker, Alfie realized, when she had learned he liked caramel popcorn—and was called *Stephen* when he was in trouble.

Poor guy, she thought, remembering EllRay when *he* got in trouble. She could almost hear some grownup shouting at Scooter. "Who ate all the caramel popcorn? Was it you, Stephen?"

"I just asked you a question, Alfie," Hanni was saying with way too much patience. She made a funny face at Lulu.

"Oh, sorry," Alfie said, surprised by the smile. "What's the question?"

"I was just *saying*, who's the boss of the Cardboard Challenge?" Hanni asked. "For our team, I mean?"

"No one," Alfie said. "Or maybe Mr. Havens will tell us who."

"This is supposed to be a free country," Hanni said, already outraged.

And they were still eating their sandwiches!

But Hanni was the kind of girl who liked to get mad in advance, just in case, Alfie had learned over the past two or three weeks. "Nothing bad has happened yet, Hanni," she said in her most soothing voice.

"But it could," Hanni insisted. She looked worried.

"Yeah," Lulu chimed in, backing up Hanni. Again!

"I guess so," Alfie said, hurrying to agree with both girls. "So maybe we should vote." Hadn't Hanni wanted to vote on what their class name should have been?

"Voting takes way too long," Hanni announced. "I'm not gonna fall behind in my work just because people want to *vote*. See, my mom says it's not too early for me to start thinking about college," she tried to explain. "And how am I gonna get into college if we sit around voting all the time?"

College? Alfie could feel her cheeks get hot. What was she supposed to say now? They were only seven! She couldn't even imagine being in third grade.

Lulu looked impressed, hearing Hanni's remark. Her straight bangs bobbed up and down as she nodded.

Phoebe just looked as if she were wishing she'd sat at a different lunch table—even a table with two or more boys sitting there.

Boys cramming food into their mouths.

Boys burping out the alphabet.

Boys having a belching contest.

Or *worse*.

"Maybe we won't *have* a boss," Alfie said, trying for a careless shrug.

"Then that boy will just grab all the good cardboard stuff," Hanni warned.

"He'd better not try," Lulu said, ready to spring to Hanni's defense—and help her get into college when the time came, too, if she possibly could.

Now it was feeling like two-against-one, Alfie thought, shocked.

And she, Alfie Jakes, was the *one*. How had *that* happened?

"We won't *let* Scooter take over and grab the good stuff, that's all," she assured both Lulu and Hanni. "There's three of us, and only one of him. Also, the parent helper and Mr. Havens will be there. Scooter can't be the boss just because he's a boy."

"Because this is a free country," Hanni said, returning to her former argument. "Alfie's right. Three-against-one. That means we can squash him!"

Alfie almost gasped, she was so surprised. "That's not what I meant," she said. "And anyway, Scooter hasn't done anything—"

"The point *is*, we'll squash him," Lulu repeated, her eyes shining with excitement. "Like you said, Alfie."

It was *Hanni* who had said the word "squash," Alfie thought, her heart thudding.

"Okay? Okay," Hanni said, taking her own quick version of a vote.

"*Yes-s-s*," Lulu agreed, giving a triumphant fist-pump as she hissed out the word.

Alfie busied herself trying to open her sweaty carton of milk with clumsy fingers.

The three first week friends were finally coming together, she told herself—even if it was in an unexpected way.

But—poor Scooter Davis, who did not have a clue that any of this was going on!

Teamwork

After lunch, Mr. Havens sorted the kids into teams as they came through the classroom door. The Cardboard Challenge teams were meeting for the first time. But Mr. Havens looked frazzled, Alfie thought. That was weird.

"Our parent helper isn't here. Maybe she had car trouble," Mr. Havens told his students. "So we're on our own this afternoon. But everything will be fine."

It was as if he was saying that last sentence to himself, Alfie thought.

Most of the kids had to sit at different tables for the challenge, not the tables where they did their normal work. "You better not mess up my space over there, or you'll be so-o-o sorry," Suzette called over to shy Alan Lewis, who was at Phoebe's table. Mr. Havens *shushed* Suzette.

Alan looked worried in spite of the *shush*.

"We should take attendance," Hanni announced to Alfie's team.

She was putting herself in charge without any vote at all!

Alfie stared hard at the cardboard objects piled in the middle of the table.

Two empty cereal boxes.

At least three cardboard tubes, one of them very long.

Lots of little gift boxes of different sizes.

One big cardboard box.

Two shoe boxes.

And two or three pieces of plain brown cardboard.

"I don't think we really need to take attendance," she objected with what she hoped was a friendly smile. "There's just four of us, Hanni. Counting you."

There's me, Alfie thought, counting on her

fingers under the table to make sure.

And Hanni, who was now frowning, in spite of that friendly smile.

And Lulu, who was smoothing down her perfect hair.

And Scooter, who was busy peeling a strip of rubber off one of his sneakers. He didn't seem to care that Hanni had basically crowned herself queen of their Cardboard Challenge.

"We just got two days to do this thing," Scooter said, looking up from his sneaker. "So we better

get going. The parent-and-guardian deal is on Friday night."

Hanni made a snorting sound. "Tell that boy it's called 'Back to School Night,' and it's not a *deal*,'" she said to Alfie without looking at Scooter.

"Why can't you tell him?" Alfie asked, confused. She knew Hanni, an only child, was shy around EllRay. But Scooter was their own age!

"The point is, we'd better start," Lulu said. "If it's okay with you, Hanni," she added hastily. "Because other kids are already making stuff. 'Build today, decorate tomorrow,' Mr. Havens told us," she reminded the others.

"That's a *great* idea, Lulu," Alfie said, beaming. "Isn't that a great idea Lulu had, Hanni?"

She was determined to keep Hanni and Lulu together, now that they seemed to like each other so much.

Leadership and cuteness.

All that was left was for her to squeeze in there somehow and add her own cricket energy, Alfie thought. And then the three perfect ingredients would be complete.

"I don't know about you, but I'm making a truck," Scooter announced, grabbing the sturdiest-looking shoebox and a couple of long cardboard tubes. "Or maybe an ATV or a tank."

"I think I'll turn two of the little boxes into a jewelry box for the locket I got in Maine last summer," Lulu said. She selected several boxes from which to choose, lining them up in front of her. "I'm putting the littlest one on top, like they do with wedding cakes," she continued. "And then tomorrow, I'm gonna paint the whole thing pink, with lots of glitter on top, and—"

"I'm making a computer," Hanni interrupted. "To show Mr. Havens and the parents and guardians what a good student I'm gonna be this year. And then I'll wrap the whole thing in foil, so it looks like silver metal. Really *expensive* silver metal," she added as if the description alone might impress the other three kids.

"Who ever heard of a silver metal computer?" Scooter asked, rolling his shoebox on a cardboard tube to test how well it moved.

Alfie could not believe her ears—or her eyes, as

she saw their heap of cardboard getting smaller by the second. "You *guys*," she finally exclaimed. "Don't you get it? Mr. Havens said we're supposed to be a team. That means we have to work *together*. Make something *together*. Just *one thing*. Team-work!"

She looked around for their teacher. There was a line of kids at the craft closet door, so he must be in there, using the paper cutter or hot glue gun.

"That's not what Mr. Havens meant," Lulu informed Alfie, reaching for a white plastic glue bottle. "He just meant we shouldn't fight. So we'll be *that* kind of team. The not-fighting kind."

"Yeah," Hanni said, squinting at the box she had chosen for her computer. "And he meant we should share the materials like a team, too."

Oh, great, Alfie thought. They were agreeing with each other *again*?

They were getting along like crazy!

What about her?

Nightmare Twist

"But—but—look over there," Alfie sputtered at Hanni, Lulu, and Scooter as she pointed to a nearby table. "That team is making something really cool. *Together*. It looks like a robot," she added, trying to tempt them to turn their heads and take a peek.

"*Ew*," Lulu said, busy with her jewelry box. "Robots."

"You can put your box of jewels next to my awesome ATV when we're done," Scooter told Lulu. "That's kind of like working together, isn't it? And then my ATV can run over that girl's computer until it's smashed flat."

"Her name's Hanni," Alfie said. "And *all* you guys should just look around, for once."

Phoebe's table was putting together a castle. It even had a drawbridge. And kids were laughing!

At another table, Bryan was blowing wadded-up balls of paper through a tube. His team was probably making a cannon or something.

Everyone was cooperating. Nobody was getting squashed. They were *teams*.

Except at Alfie's table.

"You're not the boss of us, Alfie," Lulu informed her.

"But you better get started," Hanni said, sounding almost sorry for her summer friend. "You're really falling behind. Why don't you make a poster out of one of those pieces of cardboard, Alfie?" she suggested, pointing. "It can say 'Welcome!' Then we'll all have something to show on Back to School Night. That's what we're supposed to be doing," she added, as if explaining a difficult idea to some kid who just wasn't getting it.

"Yeah," Scooter said. "Because so far, Alfie, you got nothin'."

"Nobody asked you," Lulu told him, not looking up.

"Listen. We are really supposed to be working on only *one project*," Alfie said for the third time.

"All four of us. Together," she repeated. "And we shouldn't be mean to each other," she added.

She looked around the room. Where was Mr. Havens when you needed him? Still in the craft closet?

He was huge! How could he just disappear like that?

"Yeah, right," Hanni scoffed, laughing. "Like I'm gonna wreck my grade by letting a bunch of random kids work with me on a big assignment like this. An assignment that everybody's gonna see. Even grownups. Even my mom."

Alfie blinked. Grades? *Random kids?* But she and Hanni had been pretty good friends for the past two weeks. Hanni had even given her Princess. For free! And Hanni had known every single kid at their table in first grade.

Even "that boy" Scooter Davis.

"But working together as a team is supposed to *be* the assignment," Alfie said, her voice weary. She was giving it one last shot.

"Good going, Alfie, trying to get me to help you with your challenge," Hanni said in a jokey voice.

She wrestled with a strip of duct tape so she could turn a flat, skinny box into an upright computer monitor, Alfie guessed. "Here. Hold this, would you?" Hanni asked Alfie.

"I'd like to," Alfie said, trying not to sound too huffy. "But I'm kind of busy right now, working on my own project. You know, so I can get into college."

In about a million years.

"You *are not* working on a project," Lulu said. "She isn't," she tattled to Hanni, as if Hanni couldn't see for herself. "She hasn't even started yet!"

And she and Lulu had been best friends last year, Alfie thought, frowning. But now, Lulu and Hanni were getting to be better friends with each other every second.

So her first week, second grade dream was coming true—but with a nightmare twist.

"Only half an hour more, people," Mr. Havens's voice boomed from nowhere, rolling over everyone's heads like a surprise clap of late-summer thunder. "Your projects should be built by then," he said. "We will have paint and collage materials ready for you to use tomorrow afternoon. And a parent helper will be here for sure to help you achieve your dreams."

Good luck with *that*, Alfie thought, scraping some dried glue off the table with her thumbnail. That parent helper was going to have three projects to work on at her table alone! Four, if she caved in and started making something.

They were *doomed*. All four of them.

"You better get goin' on *something*, Alfie," Scooter said, sounding worried for her. "Even if it's really lame. Just do any old thing," he advised.

"Yeah," Lulu chimed in. "Or you'll make the rest of us look bad on Friday."

"Be quiet," Scooter told her. "You're not helping."

"And you're not the boss of me—or Alfie," Lulu said, still not looking up from the boxes she was gluing together. "Or the boss of anyone. So *you* be quiet."

"*You can do it, Alfie,*" Scooter whispered.

And Alfie found herself reaching for a small white cardboard box.

A Word with Mr. Havens

"Alfie, may I have a word?" Mr. Havens said quietly as his second grade class headed out for recess that hot afternoon.

Alfie knew what he wanted to talk about. But why did it have to be with her?

"I want to ask you about your team's Cardboard Challenge," Mr. Havens said when the last second grader but Alfie had disappeared out the classroom door. "I noticed you kids were each doing your own project. But this was supposed to be a team effort, as you know. One project for each team."

"I *do* know," Alfie said. Her eyes were getting prickly and hot—a sure sign that tears were about to fall. *No, no, no*, she told herself.

Why was he telling *her* this?

"You seem to be the team leader, after all," Mr. Havens was saying, answering her silent question. "So I thought maybe you could tell me what happened."

"I'm not the leader," Alfie told him.

But she wasn't going to add anything else. She would not tattle on anyone, Alfie promised herself.

"Look. I blame myself for what happened this afternoon," Mr. Havens said.

This surprised Alfie. Teachers made mistakes—and admitted it?

"I let you guys down," Mr. Havens said. "I got carried away. I did not plan for enough help. I think I bit off more than I could chew," he added.

Huh? His mouth was huge, Alfie thought, sneaking a look at it.

So how was that even possible?

"You got stuck in the craft closet," Alfie said, hoping to make him feel better.

"Cutting up cardboard," Mr. Havens agreed,

nodding. "And using the hot glue gun to stick paper towel tubes to a castle, to make turrets," he added. "And then I was gluing tubes together—and to my shirt—for an outer space defense machine."

"The thing that looks like a cannon?" Alfie asked.

"The very one," he said, nodding.

"Not that wadded-up paper balls would work very well in outer space," Alfie said, thinking about it.

"I thought the Cardboard Challenge would be fun," Mr. Havens explained. "But we definitely needed at least *one* parent helper today, and maybe even two. I should have had a back-up plan in order. I'll organize things better next time," he assured Alfie. "And I'll arrange to have at least two helpers here tomorrow afternoon. Maybe your team's projects can still be fixed."

"It's *not my team*," she said again. "But Hanni has already made her computer," she said. "And Lulu's making a pink jewelry box with glitter on top. It's almost done. And I'm making a picture frame. And Scooter's almost finished making some kind of car."

"An ATV," Mr. Havens said. "I saw it."

Alfie blinked. He knew all that? And he still thought maybe they could "fix things tomorrow"?

A *roomful* of parent helpers couldn't save them! Not now. It was too late.

"Alfie," Mr. Havens said. "I noticed how hard you were trying to get your teammates to work together on the assignment. That counts for a lot. So don't worry."

Don't *worry*?

"Maybe I tried to remind people about the project, and maybe I didn't," Alfie said, not giving anything away. "But maybe they wouldn't listen. And who is going to tell them they did the assignment wrong?"

"I'll do it," Mr. Havens assured her. "I'll take care of it first thing tomorrow afternoon. I'm the teacher, and you're the student, Alfie," he added. "This is not your problem."

Alfie could feel her body relax a little. "But why didn't you say something today?" she asked.

"There wasn't enough time," Mr. Havens said. "And I had already explained the assignment once," he added. "Of course, I never thought I'd be stuck all afternoon with no help, or that some of you might not understand the assignment. But mistakes happen. And sometimes, the best example of something—such as teamwork—is to show what it looks like when things go wrong."

"And the example of bad teamwork is gonna be *us*?" Alfie asked, horrified.

Poor Hanni!

Poor Lulu!

Poor Scooter!

And poor her!

Four all-wrong cardboard projects, sitting there like goofballs during the art show *and* Back to School Night.

In front of everyone. Kindergartners, the principal, and parents and guardians.

Surrounded by all that really cool *teamwork*—unless Mr. Havens and his imaginary parent helpers could magically help them "fix things tomorrow."

What if things couldn't be fixed?

"But I'm truly curious about something, Alfie," Mr. Havens was saying. "You knew what the real challenge was. So why did you end up going along with the others when you knew they were wrong?"

I did it so Hanni and Lulu would still like me, Alfie thought, but didn't say.

"But—how could I do a team project all by myself?" she asked instead.

"That's a good question," Mr. Havens admitted, laughing.

"I had to do *something*," Alfie explained. "I couldn't turn in *nothing*. I kept hoping you'd come over and tell us we were doing things wrong," she added, trying not to sound too blame-y. "But you didn't."

"Outer space defense machines cannot assemble themselves," he said, shaking his head. "But as I told you, I dropped the ball."

That was basketball talk, Alfie guessed.

"How would you handle things if something like this ever happened again?" Mr. Havens asked. "Would you do anything differently, Alfie?"

Alfie thought about it. "I guess I'd make up a reason to go find you," she said at last. "You know, to ask for permission to go to the *restroom* or something," she added, whispering the word "restroom."

How embarrassing was this?

"There's a plan," he said, nodding as he smiled.

"So, are you going to flunk us on this big project?" Alfie asked, made bold by his smile. "During the very first week of second grade?" She was barely able to put the words together, they were so terrible. "Because if you put our messed-up Cardboard Challenges on display for everyone to see, Mrs. Sobel's gonna have a melt-down."

"There will be no melting-down at Back to School Night," Mr. Havens assured Alfie. "It's not a big deal. I'll explain to the parents what happened today, and how it was my fault things went wrong. We can all learn from this, Alfie," he added. "Myself included. It takes *time* for teamwork to happen."

"It is a big deal at Hanni's house," Alfie told him. "You should see it over there, Mr. Havens. Everything's perfect—in every single room. Mrs. Sobel even has matching cookies stacked up straight in fancy glass jars," she explained, trying to give Mr. Havens an example.

Alfie had spent every other day at Hanni's house during the last three weeks of summer. She loved looking at the things in each perfect room at the Sobels' house, but she was always relieved when she went home.

She could breathe deeper, somehow, in her own relaxed and cozy house.

If the parent helpers couldn't fix things tomorrow, Alfie did not think Mrs. Sobel was going to appreciate having Hanni's pretend computer displayed as a bad example of teamwork on Friday night—no matter what Mr. Havens thought.

Sometimes teachers just didn't *get* parents! Not some parents, anyway.

"There's always hope, Miss Jakes," Mr. Havens said, giving her a big, muscular smile. "You're a loyal friend, and we still have tomorrow. I'll talk to your team first thing in the afternoon."

He was right. The Cardboard Challenge wasn't over yet, Alfie told herself as she slipped out the door and hurried to the girls' restroom before it was time for class to start again.

There was still tomorrow.

12

Scramble

Alfie slid the note under EllRay's bedroom door about ten minutes after the family finished dinner and the dishes. Tiny Princess made a furry, purry figure-eight around her ankles as Alfie waited for her brother to notice it.

"I am in troble," Alfie's note read.

Because *yes*, she and EllRay sometimes got on each other's nerves.

And *yes*, he was often too busy with his friends to hang out with her anymore.

And *yes*, he had refused to help her with the Cardboard Challenge.

But they had always been a team.

Alfie sank down on the hallway floor outside EllRay's room. She pulled Princess onto her lap and waited. She knew her sixth-grader brother was either busy plotting how to *rule*, whatever that meant, or he was doing his amazingly complicated sixth grade homework.

Dividing specks of dust, maybe.

Wasn't she, Alfie, supposed to be doing her own "Word Scramble" worksheet that very minute? She should be figuring out how to put together five or six floating words so they made a real sentence that could sit without embarrassment on a line of notebook paper.

"The boy throws the ball," instead of *"boy The ball throws the."*

An answering note slid back out to her, and Princess pounced on it. "No," Alfie whispered, laughing. "Give it here, kitty."

She unfolded EllRay's note.

"Knock three times, then count to ten, then come in," it read.

Alfie chewed her lip for a second. "I don't know this first word yet," she called through the door. "What am I supposed to do three times before I count to ten?"

"Knock," EllRay yelled back.

"Oh. I think you spelled it wrong, but okay," Alfie said. She could do that.

Knock. Knock. Knock.

One—two—three—four—five—six—seven—eight—nine—ten.

Open the door.

Her brother sat with his back against the bed, an open notebook on the floor next to him. He scratched his fingers on the floor, and Princess tottered over. She was part of their team now, too, Alfie thought, smiling.

Their cute mascot, maybe.

"What kind of trouble?" EllRay asked. "It's only the first week of school. I gotta say, I'm surprised," he added, teasing.

"Don't joke," Alfie said. "And *please* don't tell Mom or Dad. This is serious, and they'll find out soon enough. Remember the Cardboard Challenge I told you about last night?" she asked. "That teamwork project you wouldn't help me with?"

"Uh-huh," EllRay said, not looking at all guilty as he tickled Princess's tummy.

And Alfie told her brother the story of that terrible afternoon.

"Where was Coach during all this?" EllRay asked. "Mr. Havens, I mean?"

"In the craft closet," Alfie reported. "But later on, he seemed to know everything that happened."

"He's like that on the playground, too," EllRay told her, nodding. "He's Stealth-Dude out there during basketball practice. He sees all and hears all. He catches every little mistake. So, how did it end?" he asked.

"Mr. Havens said he'd talk to the other kids on my team tomorrow afternoon," Alfie said. "He wasn't really worried at all," she added, frowning. "He said 'mistakes happen.' He's treating the whole thing like it's some weird science experiment."

"Yeah," EllRay said. "Sometimes he lets kids goof up—just to prove a point. Especially if they didn't listen in the first place."

"But now, my team only has one more day—an hour, really—to get the project right," Alfie told him. "Because today was building day, see, and tomorrow is decorating day," she explained.

"Huh."

"But what do you think I should do tomorrow *morning*?" Alfie asked. "Something? Anything?"

"The way I see it, you have two choices," EllRay said. "One, you could tell the other kids what Mr. Havens said about them doing the project wrong," he told her. "Or two, you could *not* tell them what he said. Just let him do it in the afternoon, like he said."

"I like number two," Alfie said. "I already told them the right thing once," she added, "and no-body listened. If I tell them again, Hanni and Lulu might say I think I'm so great. And anyway, no matter what he says, it's too late for us to build a new teamwork project together *and* have time to decorate it. No matter how much help we get. Not with just one hour left tomorrow."

"I guess you're right," EllRay said, stroking the now-sleeping kitten curled up on his open notebook.

"But if I *don't* tell them what he said about teamwork," Alfie said, trying to work out this real-life scramble as she spoke, "and if we don't have time to fix things, then I will end up turning in a wrong project too. And on Back to School Night, Mom and Dad will think I didn't know any better. They'll be so embarrassed."

Especially her dad, Alfie thought. He was super-interested in having EllRay and her doing well in school.

"They'll survive," EllRay said, laughing. "I've embarrassed them a lot worse."

"But instead of being the All-Stars," Alfie said, "our team will be the *No-Stars* if I turn in a wrong assignment, too. Not that I could do a team project all by myself. I'm just one kid. But even if it's wrong," she added, cheering herself up, "I'll still have my special first week, second grade friends. Hanni and Lulu will still like me."

I hope, she added silently.

"Sorry I couldn't help," EllRay said, shrugging.

"Oh, I don't know," Alfie said, flashing her big brother a smile. "For some weird reason, I usually feel better after talking to you, EllRay. Thanks."

"You're welcome?" he said, turning his reply into a confused question.

But then he smiled at her, too.

Teamwork!

Good-night Cuddle

An hour later, Alfie was freshly showered and sitting up in bed coloring as she waited for her dad. She had already said good night to her mom. She wished Princess was there—but Princess had decided to sleep in EllRay's room tonight.

"Oh well," Alfie murmured.

"Oh well, what?" her dad said, slipping into her room.

"Oh well, I have to share Princess," she explained. "But I don't mind."

Dr. Jakes perched on the end of Alfie's bed. He was tall and thin, and his glasses glittered in the darkened room. He straightened his daughter's blanket and gently brushed his big hand across her brow. "My second-grader," he said, sounding proud. "Did you finish your homework, Cricket?"

"Mm-hmm," she said, nodding. "It was just a couple of worksheets. I think Mr. Havens is busy thinking about Back to School Night on Friday. But you and Mom don't have to go if you don't want to," she added, inspired. "I can tell you what he's going to say."

"Are you kidding?" her dad said. "We wouldn't miss it for the world! I want to see for myself what's going on with Mr. Havens and the All-Stars," he added.

"So you heard about that," Alfie said, and she sighed. Her eyes wanted to close as her father spoke, but she had to stay alert, she warned herself. There was something she needed to say. "That means you're going to be the one visiting my class, right?" she asked. "And Mom is going to EllRay's room this year?"

It was complicated for parents when they had two kids going to the same school on Back to School Night, Alfie knew.

"For the most part," her dad told her. "But of

course your mom and I will meet both your teachers. I hope there will be lots of work up on the walls," he said, smiling in the dark.

"It's only Wednesday," Alfie warned him. "The first week of school. We haven't *done* very much work yet. In fact, I haven't learned one new thing," she added, scowling. "Maybe you should ask for your money back. Or stay home."

"I'm not worried," her dad said, laughing. "There's a little time left in the school year, I think."

"As long as I'm trying. Right, Dad?" Alfie asked, hoping to plant this idea in his brainy head.

"Mmm?" he asked, sounding as if he were away somewhere, lost in his own scientific thoughts. Geology was about everything that made up planet Earth, Alfie knew by now, so those thoughts could keep him pretty busy.

"Just as long as I try, then that's okay," Alfie said, repeating her secret message in a slightly different way.

"Well, trying is certainly important," her father said, thinking about it. "But I believe that both you and EllRay know that your mother and I expect a little more of you than just that."

"But trying is a big *part* of anything, right?" Alfie asked. "Because nobody can be perfect all the time."

She pictured her father on Back to School Night, peering down at her puny cardboard frame as a tiny photograph of Princess stared back at him. "Teamwork!" Mr. Havens would be saying as her father's brow wrinkled in concern, seeing this solitary effort. Could it *be* any more opposite?

He might come home disappointed in her!

The worst.

"I don't expect you to be perfect, Alfie," her dad said, his voice rumbly and deep. "You're not worried about that, are you?"

"Not *that*," Alfie murmured. "Not exactly."

But there was a big difference between perfection, she thought, and doing your first assignment all wrong. Her dad wouldn't know any of the complicated details about how that had happened.

About the parent helper who might have had car trouble.

About the long line at the craft closet.

About Mr. Havens's goofy "mistakes happen" attitude.

About the parent helpers who probably wouldn't be able to fix things tomorrow.

"I'm sure everything at Back to School Night will be just fine," Alfie's dad said, getting ready to kiss her cheek and leave. "Your mother and I will come home on Friday night as proud as peacocks—of both our children."

"But if you *don't* come home proud, at least you know we tried," Alfie reminded him. "Because everyone makes mistakes, Dad. They *happen*."

"I know that, Alfie," her father told her, sounding a little bewildered. "Now, stop worrying, and go to sleep. Okay? Can you do that for me? Because tomorrow is another day."

Grownups were always saying stuff like that, Alfie thought scooching down under the covers.

"I can *try* to sleep," she said, driving home her point in what she hoped was a sneaky but clever way.

"You *try*, then, Cricket," her dad said, grazing his lips across her cheek. It was his version of a goodnight kiss. "Sleep tight."

Hah, Alfie thought, watching a pie-slice of golden ceiling light grow skinny as he closed her bedroom door behind him. Just—*hah*.

She was going to sleep loose, not tight. Loose—and worried.

14

The Perfect S'more

On Thursday morning, Alfie could feel the difference in temperature at once when she went outside. "That's better," she whispered as she climbed into her mom's car for carpool.

According to her brother EllRay's theory, it would either be hot today, or hot-hot. But not weird-hot.

Hanni was full of chatter about her cardboard project during the ride to school, but Alfie didn't say a word. She would leave everything to Mr. Havens.

Once they got to school, the morning went by so fast that she didn't have time to worry much about that afternoon's decorating session. Mr. Havens's class whizzed through Shared Reading, Writing Workshop, and morning recess as if they'd been in second grade for months, not just a few days.

Even math went by fast. Alfie was calling it "Money Math," because money had been the theme of the arithmetic they'd done so far. Today, Suzette Monahan had a mini-meltdown during the "Can I Buy It?" lesson when she learned that she did not have enough pretend money to buy the pretend snack she wanted.

But apart from that, the All-Stars had it *down*, Mr. Havens assured them.

Now it was time for lunch, and to Alfie's joy it was cool enough for them to eat outside. "Wait for me," Phoebe was telling Arletty at the cubby room door. "Can we eat together? You too, Alfie, if you want," she added. A crowd of noisy, hungry kids churned around them, but Phoebe's voice was friendly and warm.

Phoebe could be a character in one of her mother's books, Alfie thought, watching the girl's golden hair catch the light. Some princess's daughter, maybe.

Alfie wondered what it would be like to have easy hair like Phoebe's. Just brush-and-go, she guessed. But she knew she would miss the special time her mom spent with her each day, doing her hair. Not the detangling part, but everything else.

"Maybe I can," she said to Phoebe with a smile.

But it wouldn't be today, because this lunch was Alfie's last chance to play with Hanni and Lulu before that afternoon's dreaded decorating session. She needed somehow to super-glue the three of them together for good. She wanted to stay on their sweet side so they would end up fitting together perfectly—like a three-piece puzzle.

After that, it would be Hanni, Lulu, and Alfie forever.

Leadership, cuteness, and energy. Win, win, win!

Hanni and Lulu had already gone outside together to the picnic tables, along with Suzette Monahan and a couple of other girls in their class. Alfie hurried after them.

* * *

Like most kids, Alfie finished her lunch as quickly as possible. She always wanted more time to play. But when playtime came, instead of choosing what seemed to her to be the most fun thing to do, Alfie looked to see what Hanni and Lulu were doing.

Because today, she needed to do *that*.

Hanni and Lulu were down in the sunken play area, perched on a circle of upright logs that had been turned into outdoor chairs. The circle had been installed around what the kids called their invisible campfire. This was one of Oak Glen Primary School's new "nature features," they'd been told the first day of school.

The second grade girls had claimed it right away.

Alfie liked activities in the running-and-jumping family much better than perching, but *whatever*, she told herself, remembering her goal.

"Hi, guys," she said, slipping into the circle of girls and taking a seat.

"Hey," Suzette said, welcoming her.

"We need marshmallows," Hanni announced, staring at the sandy area in front of her.

This was a good sign, Alfie thought, excited— because marshmallows were one of the three ingredients in s'mores! And s'mores were her private symbol for what might become her three-girl, second grade friendship with Hanni and Lulu. "Yeah, but they'd never let us build a fire here," Suzette said, shaking her head.

Hanni shrugged. "We could eat 'em raw," she said.

"I love s'mores all three ways," Alfie chimed in. "Raw, toasted, or burned. They're the perfect food."

"Yeah," another girl said. "You can't wreck 'em unless they plop in the dirt."

"But I think marshmallows are supposed to be bad for you," Suzette said, frowning.

"Maybe, if that's all you ever ate," Alfie said, hoping to make everyone happy.

Lulu had been busy fiddling with her flowered headband, trying to get it just right. But now she spoke, changing the subject. "I don't like the way Mr. Havens sneaks up on you," she said.

Alfie was startled. Was Lulu talking about her meeting with Mr. Havens during recess yesterday?

Don't talk about the Cardboard Challenge. Don't talk about the Cardboard Challenge, she reminded herself.

"Sneaks up on everyone," Lulu said. She had been scolded that morning during Writing Workshop for peeking at a little round mirror she had tucked into her notebook, Alfie remembered. It was clear that Mr. Havens's words—a mild correction—still stung.

"He's so strict," another girl agreed.

"It's strange how Mr. Havens sees and hears every little thing," Alfie admitted.

"Yeah. That's what I was *saying*," Lulu told her. "And it's weird, because he's so big! How can Mr. Havens be sneaky and gigantic at the same time? That's not fair."

"I bet he eats a ton of food," Hanni said, thinking aloud.

Mr. Havens "bit off more than he could chew," Alfie thought. He said so himself!

"A *ton*," she replied as if she were seconding a motion during a class election.

Around them, kids were swinging, sliding, climbing, or pretend-crawling like crabs up the grassy slopes that surrounded the sunken play area, Alfie saw. Her legs almost twitched, they wanted so much to run and play with them. But she stayed put. "Your headband looks good," she told Lulu, who immediately adjusted it again.

"Thanks," Lulu said, granting her a smile. "It's new."

"We should run," Hanni announced, as if she had been reading Alfie's mind. Alfie could have hugged her, she was so happy to hear those words. After all, she thought, the weather was perfect! A breeze was blowing, and puffy white clouds skidded across the sky.

"Or we could hold hands and skip," Alfie said, inspired. "We used to do that in the olden days."

Last year, she remembered. In first grade.

"What, all of us?" Hanni asked, a smile and two dimples appearing on her face.

"Because I've skipped with one girl before,"

Lulu said, as if finishing the same sentence. "But not with a whole *bunch* of girls. Is that even possible? It sounds dangerous."

"It might be awesome," Alfie said, tempting her. "And you and your headband would look really cute doing it, Lulu."

By now, the girls were on their feet, shaking their legs in preparation for the group-skip. Alfie reached out her hand, and Hanni took it.

Lulu took her other hand, to Alfie's delight, and within moments, a few other girls had joined them.

"Somebody's gotta yell 'Start,' or we'll just drag each other down and mess up our outfits," Suzette said from somewhere down the line.

"I think it should be Hanni," Alfie said, because of her friend's leadership skills. Sure, some girls called Hanni bossy, but—

"Start!" Hanni cried, and she took off skipping, right leg first.

There were a few early stumbles, but then the line of girls was off and skipping—across the sand, past the swings and the two slides, one straight

and one curly, and then up the sloping path.

Skippety-*skip*! Skippety-*skip*! Skippety-*skip*!

The hill slowed the laughing girls down a bit, and a couple of them staggered and let go as the girls neared the picnic tables.

By the time they started heading down the slope again, skipping faster now, it was just Alfie, Hanni, and Lulu.

This was awesome, Alfie thought, her heart soaring. *Yes-s-s!*

And when they were on flat ground again, Alfie felt as if she were rising higher into the air with every skip that she took. It was as though she had no weight at all! She seemed to hover in the air at the top of each skip—like an Alfie balloon.

All *three* of them were floating like balloons, Alfie thought, awed.

It was *perfection*.

And then, of course, the buzzer sounded, and the magic moment came to an end. But Alfie knew that her first week, second grade wish had come true—and the three ingredients finally had come together to form the perfect s'more.

Their friendship could survive anything, Alfie thought.

"If we can get through the decorating session this afternoon, that is," she whispered to herself.

15

No Harm, No Foul

"Finally," Scooter Davis said as Alfie, Hanni, and Lulu bounced into class moments before the final buzzer sounded. "Our parent helper lady already brought over the projects, only you guys weren't here. She had a funny look on her face, too," he added. "And she said Mr. Havens wants to talk to us."

"About what?" Hanni asked, frowning as she fiddled with her cardboard computer.

"How should I know?" Scooter asked, shrugging.

"I have arrived," Mr. Havens announced to Alfie's table. His deep voice was easy to hear over the room's *buzz, buzz-z, buzz-z-z*, the excited sound of kids making art—with three parent helpers to assist them today.

Great, Alfie thought, listening to her heartbeat pounding in her ears. Now she had to pretend to be surprised by what Mr. Havens was going to say.

Life was getting complicated.

"Is this about Alfie not starting her project until really late yesterday?" Lulu asked Mr. Havens. "Because we tried to get her to start earlier, but—"

"No," Mr. Havens interrupted. "It's about all four of you getting off track with the Cardboard Challenge. This is a teamwork project, guys. *One project per team.* Open your eyes. Look around."

Lulu, Hanni, and Scooter stared at the other kids' projects, but Alfie gazed down at her small cardboard picture frame. It was as if she were hoping the picture of Princess inside the frame might start meowing at her—telling her that everything was going to be just *purr*-fect, and not to worry.

"Shoot," Scooter said, scowling at his ATV. "We did it all wrong."

"You are not being graded on this assign-

ment," Mr. Havens assured them. "And it was my fault there weren't enough helpers yesterday. But today, you will have your own parent helper—just for this table alone."

"But what for-r-r-r?" Hanni said, turning the last word into a wail of despair. "It's too late to make things right! And Back to School Night is tomorrow!"

"I know," Scooter said, getting an idea. "We

could glue all our projects together and make, like, a giant float! Because Hanni's computer could go on top of my ATV, see? And Lulu's glitter box could go on the computer, and Alfie's little picture could—"

"I don't want my jewel box glued to anyone else's stuff," Lulu said, stamping her foot—which wasn't easy to do, sitting down.

"I'll let you work that out with your assigned parent helper," Mr. Havens said. "You kids can either finish up your projects as they are, or you can find a way to turn them into a team project. It's entirely up to you. No harm, no foul," he added, confusing at least three of the kids.

And then he was gone.

Lulu turned to Alfie. "Don't you dare say 'I told you so,'" she said, frowning. "Even though I guess you did."

Alfie's body grew stiff. "I would never—"

"Alfie didn't say a word, Lulu," Hanni said, sticking up for Alfie. "And she did the project wrong, too."

"Only because we *made* her do it wrong," Scooter said, thinking about it.

"I decided that's how I wanted to do it," Alfie said, not explaining why.

"And here I am again," a grownup lady said, almost skidding up to their table. She was so full of energy that she nearly fizzed. "I'm Mrs. Lewis," the woman said, brushing at some glitter that was stuck to her cheek. "Alan's mom. So, what's the final decision about these projects?" she asked. "Mr. Havens said there was talk of sticking them together. And I'm pretty good with a hot glue gun."

"But I don't want to do that," Lulu said. "Mr. Havens told us we're not getting graded on them, didn't he? And I want to take my jewel box home once Back to School Night is over. I can't do that if it's in the middle of some weird art *sandwich*."

"So that's that," Alfie announced, even though Hanni still looked worried. She was probably thinking about what her persnickety mom was going to say, Alfie guessed.

"That's not *really* that," Scooter argued. "We could still glue *three* of the projects together." He pointed to Hanni's computer, to his ATV, and to

Alfie's picture frame. "I mean, look at the other guys' stuff," he added, gesturing around the room. "At least then, our project would look right. More like teamwork, I mean."

The robot construction was now being painted bright blue by four kids.

Phoebe and Alan's team's castle had a draw-bridge and turrets. Pointed flags were being strung up.

And Bryan's team's space weapon looked ready to take on all hostile alien enemies. The five team members swarmed around it like ants at a picnic table.

The last team had made a hamster run, it looked like. It featured tunnels, a connected rest area that even the fussiest rodent would enjoy, and a ramp leading up to what one boy was calling the invisible hamster's "media room."

Maybe there would be a real hamster inside the run on Back to School Night!

"So cool," Alfie couldn't help but say, admiring it.

"Be quiet, *you*," Lulu said to Alfie. "And you too, *Stephen*," she added.

"That's not necessary," Mrs. Lewis said, her

voice friendly but crisp. "Mr. Havens says you are each free to make your own decision."

"So we won't really get blamed," Alfie said, half-explaining things to Hanni.

"We'll get a little bit blamed," Hanni murmured.

"Decision time," Mrs. Lewis said, tapping her watch.

Lulu cradled her arms around her jewelry box. "I could use some pink paint and silver glitter, maybe," she told Mrs. Lewis.

"And I need some shiny yellow paint for my ATV," Scooter said, as if he had just made up his mind to keep his project separate from the rest. "And I gotta have something to draw stripes with," he added. "Or maybe flames?"

"I guess I need silver paper and glue," Hanni said. "And a black marker that's not gonna smear on shiny paper."

"And what about you?" Mrs. Lewis asked Alfie. "What do you need, honey?"

I need not to cry, Alfie thought, watching Hanni and Lulu work together—and picturing the expression on her dad's face on Back to School Night. "Just a little paint for the frame, and three dabs of glue for the back of my kitty's picture," she said.

They were now so far behind that kids at other tables were looking at them, Alfie noticed, her cheeks hot with embarrassent. Arletty and Phoebe were trying to catch her eye. They smiled, encouraging her.

"Time to finish," Mr. Havens said, looming over them again as suddenly as Bigfoot popping up in a forest, Alfie thought. She had seen a TV show about this mysterious creature last summer and been much impressed.

Fake, EllRay had announced. But Alfie didn't care. She loved poor lonely Bigfoot. She hoped he had lots of forest friends—and that they never quarreled.

"Good," Mr. Havens said as Mrs. Lewis hurried to their table with the needed art supplies. "Now, the four of you may have five extra minutes to complete your projects while your classmates begin their afternoon recess." he continued in a that's-that tone of voice. "So, finish up, All-Stars."

"Thanks a lot," Hanni muttered, but not quietly enough.

Whoa.

But Hanni was a tiny bit scared of her mom, Alfie knew. Maybe that was making her reckless and rude.

"Don't worry, Hanni," Mr. Havens said quietly, in spite of the girl's display of bad manners. "I'll explain to the parents and guardians just how proud I am of *every single project*. It has been a memorable first week, hasn't it?" he asked. "Full of learning experiences, too—for us all," he added before stalking off to another table on his long, basketball-playing legs.

The week had been a little *too* memorable, Alfie thought with a shaky sigh. In fact, it had been like a roller coaster. Up, up, up—and then *down*.

What had happened to lunch-time's dream-come-true?

Gone, as if it had never existed. Just like a *real* dream.

Poof.

And where was that perfect s'more she had imagined?

It had vanished.

Or had it?

16

A Field Trip down the Hall

After lunch on Friday, Mr. Haven's All-Stars hurried to get their projects ready for that afternoon's art show, and for Back to School Night. Their guests this afternoon would be Oak Glen Primary School's kindergartners—and Principal James.

Great, Alfie thought, making a face. Now, their principal—king of the school, basically—would think she was a kid who did not know how to follow instructions.

He would probably put her name on some *list*.

"Mr. Havens," Arletty said, raising her hand even though they were all standing around the long display table at the back of the classroom.

"Yes, Arletty?" their teacher said.

"Is this art show really supposed to be a treat for those little kids?" she asked, worried. "Because I heard some of them talking at lunch, and they think they're going on a field trip."

"Yeah," Scooter said, cracking up as he poked Bryan in the ribs with his elbow. "A field trip down the hall. That's so lame!"

"This is more like a field trip *rehearsal* for them," Mr. Havens said after giving Scooter a look that quieted him at once.

"Like a visit to 'the bigs'?" Bryan asked, and he stood a little straighter, proud.

"Something like that," Mr. Havens said, arranging the fancy labels in front of each project—even the four from Alfie's team.

But Alfie couldn't even think about her project. Instead, she found herself brooding about her friends.

No one was mad at her, true. And no other disaster had occurred.

But *abracadabra*! And not in a good way.

Because Hanni Sobel, Alfie's neighbor and late-summer friend, had wanted to hang out with Lulu and Suzette instead of Alfie this morning, even though Alfie and Hanni had chattered like two colorful parakeets during the ride to school.

And Lulu Marino, Alfie's best friend in first grade, seemed to be drifting away from her forever—like a polar bear on an ice floe.

There went the three perfect ingredients, Alfie thought—*gloomph,* right down the garbage disposal.

"Your project looks so cute," Suzette Monahan was whispering to Lulu.

"Thanks," Lulu said. She drew a finger under her perfectly-straight bangs, making them swing like shiny fringe. "I like it."

"C'mon, Alfie," Phoebe Miller said, moving in to give her a gentle nudge. "The kindergarten kids are here, and we're supposed to sit down and look friendly. Or not scary, anyway. Arletty saved us some seats."

"Okay," Alfie said, wondering if Hanni, Lulu, and Suzette would be sitting nearby.

Awkward.

The kindergartners trooped in two-by-two, many of them holding hands. They looked so small!

Principal James followed, looking enormous in comparison.

"Now, don't knock over the art," the kindergartners' pretty teacher sang out.

"*What* art?" a little boy asked. He looked around the All-Stars' room, puzzled.

"Hands in your pockets, Marty, if you don't want to hold Sasha's hand," his teacher told him as he spotted the space weapon with its ammunition—cotton balls, today—piled nearby.

Again, probably *not* very useful in outer space battles, Alfie told herself, shaking her head.

Mr. Havens caught her eye and grinned.

"*Co-o-o-l*," Marty was saying, his eyes wide. He clearly wanted to get his hands on it and start blasting aliens from other galaxies left, right, and center.

Ka-pow! Blam, blam, blammo!

"Watch him, or he'll wreck it," Bryan muttered under his breath.

"I don't want to hold *his* hand, either," the tiny pigtailed girl who must have been Sasha said. "He's *gwoss!*"

Principal James cleared his throat—probably trying not to laugh, Alfie thought.

In spite of herself, she smiled. She used to talk like that, she remembered. Well, she didn't remember, exactly, but she'd been told.

"*EllWay*," her parents said she used to call her brother.

"I'll bet he *is* gross," Arletty whispered to Alfie, giggling.

"I think I saw him pick his nose yesterday near the curly slide," Phoebe reported.

"*Ew-w-w*," Alfie and Arletty chorused softly.

Mr. Havens introduced Principal James to all the kids. Then Alfie's teacher gave a speech to the wriggling kindergartners about teamwork, art, and recycling cardboard. Alfie wasn't sure how much of it sank in. The kids looked pretty baffled.

But then, as the kindergartners bumbled out the door, Mr. Havens gave each one a cute eraser from a basket he held in one humongous hand.

That perked them up, Alfie noticed, still smiling.

"This is *fwee*?" Sasha asked, unable to believe her luck. "I can't *wait* 'til second gwade!"

Take your time, Sasha, Alfie wanted to tell the little girl. *Enjoy the fake-y field trips and free erasers while you can.*

Because being in 'the bigs' could be *tough*.

Perfect Together

"Hey, EllRay," Alfie said a few hours later, poking her head into the family room. Their parents had just left for Back to School Night.

Princess was asleep atop her new carpeted cat tower. She was tiny, but her purring filled the room.

"Huh?" EllRay said. He pressed pause on the console of the kid-version of his current favorite video game. He looked away from the TV screen, where three drooling, gauze-wrapped zombies were now also frozen mid-lurch. "Is the pizza here already?" he asked, his eyes lighting up. "And where's Bree?"

Bree was their sixteen-year-old babysitter, though neither Alfie nor EllRay liked to use that word. "Is the teenager coming over tonight?" was how they liked to describe her.

"No pizza yet," Alfie reported. "We just phoned it in five minutes ago. Three different kinds. Pineapple and ham for Bree, all-meat for you, and just-plain-cheese for me. And Bree's talking to her boyfriend in the living room," she added. "I think they're fighting," she whispered.

"What?" EllRay said. "Her boyfriend's in the living room? And you were listening in?"

"I wasn't," Alfie objected, fibbing a little. "She's on her cell. But can I talk to you for a second?"

This might be her only chance tonight, Alfie figured. Because once their pizzas arrived, any hope of privacy would be gone. Their time would be filled with gobbling down pizza, then watching a pre-approved movie.

After that, she would have to deal with with her mom and dad, once they got home from Back to School Night.

"Yeah, I know I did the teamwork assignment wrong."

"Yeah, I learned my lesson about paying attention."

"Yeah, I know I'm supposed to say 'yes,' not yeah."

"You wanna talk to me?" EllRay asked, setting aside his console with some reluctance after giving it a loving pat. "Talk about what, though? Your cardboard project, or those special friends of yours? Lanni and Hulu, right?"

"Quit it," Alfie said. "It's Hanni and Lulu. And you were listening to me that night?" she asked, amazed.

"Sometimes I can't help it," her brother teased. "It's like this tiny mosquito buzzing in my ear. *Nzz. Nzzzz. Nzzzzzz,*" he whined, darting pinched fingers toward her as he imitated the annoying sound.

"Quit it," she said, swatting his hand away. "Yeah, it's about Hanni and Lulu," she said. "See, I wanted the three of us to be best friends forever—because we were perfect together. Like *s'mores,*" she tried to explain. "I tried everything I could to make it happen."

"But it blew up in your face, right?" her brother asked.

"Yeah, only not so violent," Alfie said, thinking

about it. "It was more like, *pyu-u-u-u*," she said, making the sound of a balloon losing its air.

"And Lulu used to be your best friend last year," EllRay reminded her.

"I *know*," Alfie said, relieved that her brother understood the unfairness of the situation. "And the two of them are hanging out with *Suzette Monahan* now. So *they're* the three special friends," she concluded, shaking her head. "And the whole idea was my invention! My *plan*."

"But you can't plan *people*," EllRay told her. "Because other people have plans, too. And their plans are usually different."

"Only now, my first week of second grade is over," Alfie said. "And it's ruined. I tried my hardest, but everything went wrong. And I ended up with *zero friends*."

"I thought Mom said that some girl named Phoebe invited you over to play at her house tomorrow afternoon," EllRay said.

"Yeah, Phoebe's *mom* did," Alfie admitted. "She called our mom after school. But Phoebe is brand-new, from somewhere in Arizona. I don't know anything about her. And she wasn't part of my plan."

"How could she have been, if she's new?" Ell-Ray said. "You didn't even know her before school started. Look. Forget your plan," he advised.

"Also, there's only one of Phoebe," Alfie said, ignoring her brother's advice as she finished her thought. "So how can we ever be the three best friends?"

But—there was always Arletty, Alfie reminded herself suddenly, remembering the fun moments the three of them had had together this past week.

Phoebe, Arletty, and Alfie. That could be a pretty cool group of three!

Arletty was usually busy on weekends with church stuff, but she was at school all during the week, Alfie thought, brightening.

"Just let things happen. That's my advice to you," EllRay said.

Alfie tried to look as if she were paying attention, but her stomach growled. "Where are our pizzas, anyway?" she asked her brother.

Ding! The Jakes's doorbell sounded as she spoke.

"I'll get it," Bree called from the living room.

"Because she thinks the pizza guy is so cute," Alfie told EllRay. "That's why."

"I've got the money right here," Bree sang out. "You guys get out some plates and stuff ready in the kitchen, okay?"

"Like I need a plate to eat a pizza," EllRay scoffed, speaking to Alfie. "Dad says that us guys like to eat pizza with the hot cardboard box sitting on our laps."

"*Dad* says that?" Alfie asked, laughing at the thought of their father—always so fresh, so perfectly dressed, so serious—eating pizza that way. Who knew? "Well, I'm using a plate," she said, heading toward the kitchen—with Princess scampering close behind. "I don't want to get in any more trouble with Mom and Dad than I'm already in—by not minding Bree, or by dumping melted cheese all over the floor."

"I don't think you'll be in too much trouble tonight, Alf," EllRay told her, close behind. "Only a little. It's just the first week of school, after all. And it's not that big a deal, goofing up a team assignment. The worst person on the team usually takes care of that. And that will never be you."

"But Mom and Dad are gonna want to talk about it, for sure," Alfie said over her shoulder.

"Well, *duh*," her brother agreed. "But you can take it, can't you?" her asked, cheering her on in advance. "You're pretty tough," he said, meaning it.

"Absolutely," she agreed. "I'll pretend I'm falling asleep, if I have to."

"Classic," he said, laughing.

And the kitchen table was set—in a casual, pizza-night kind of way—by the time Bree bounced into the room with the stacked pizza boxes balanced in her arms.

In the Dark

"You amaze me," Alfie's mom said later that night, stroking her daughter's forehead in the dark.

"Why?" Alfie asked. "Because I took my shower and brushed my teeth before you guys got home tonight?"

"That," Mrs. Jakes said, laughing, "and how big you've gotten—so *fast*."

"I'm still a shrimp," Alfie pointed out, pretend-arguing as she struggled to keep her eyes open. "And face it, Mom. I messed up that Cardboard Challenge thing pretty bad. Is Dad disappointed in me?"

"Of course not," her mom said. "We understood what had happened after Mr. Havens pulled us aside and explained things."

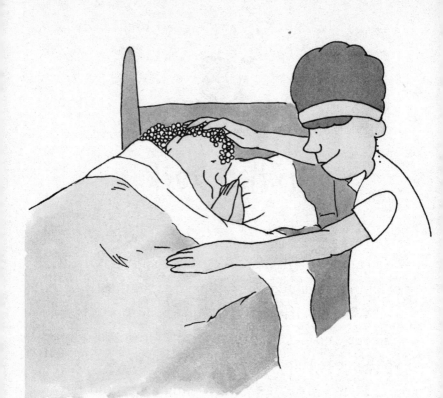

"He's pretty cool after all," Alfie admitted.

"How would *you* explain what happened, sweetie?" her mom asked, curious.

"I guess Mr. Havens was trying to plan too much stuff for one day, like he told me" Alfie said. "Kind of the way I was trying to plan my friends,

I guess. See, with me, it began when I got the jitters the day before school started, remember?" she asked, thinking back to last Sunday. "Having a friend-plan made me feel better about starting second grade, for some reason. But EllRay says you can't plan *people*," she added with a sigh.

"He's right," Mrs. Jakes said, laughing in the dark. "People will trip up your plans every single time."

"But I *like* people, Mom," Alfie murmured sleepily.

"I know you do," her mother said. "And people like you."

"Not last week, they didn't," Alfie said, shaking her head. "Not Hanni and Lulu."

"That will change," her mom told her. "I promise."

"Maybe it will, and maybe it won't," Alfie said, sounding doubtful. "But it could be like a roller coaster, right?" she added, her eyes closing. "Maybe things *will* get fun again with Hanni and Lulu someday."

"A roller coaster is exactly what primary school

friendships can be like," her mom said. "Good for you, Alfie, for figuring that out. Meanwhile," she added, "you've made at least one brand-new friend this week."

Phoebe Miller.

"Even though that wasn't what I planned," Alfie said. "She does seem pretty chill, though," she added, using one of her big brother's favorite expressions. "Really nice, in fact. And Arletty likes her, too."

"There you go, then," her mom said, getting ready to leave the room.

"Wait a minute, okay?" Alfie asked, reaching for her mother in the dark.

"Did you want to talk about something else, sweetie?" her mom asked.

"Nuh-uh," Alfie murmured, shaking her head again. "But can you just sit with me? You don't have to say anything."

Because honestly, Alfie thought, she didn't think her brain—or her heart—could hold one more thing after this goofy first week of school.

Not a plan, not a thought, not a feeling.

Alfie just wanted to be alone with her mother for a while. Her mom *never* changed.

"Love you, Mom," Alfie whispered into the night.

"I love *you*, Alfie," her mother said.

And she settled in for a nice long stay.

Join **Alfie**
on absolutely all
her adventures!

✳ ✳ ✳

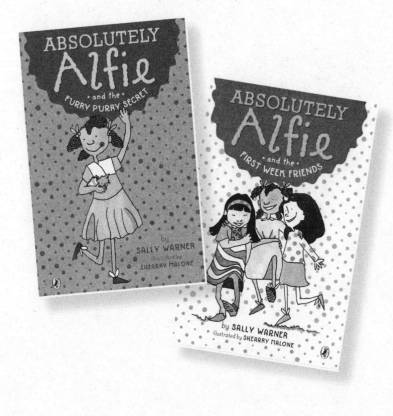